Edited by Matthew A. Clarke

This book is gratefully dedicated to my parents, who put up with me returning to and squatting in their house when the world fell down during Covid. Thank you for always being there.

Cthulhu Fishing off the Iraq Nebula

Chris Meekings

Planet Bizarro Press

1

IN SPACE, NO ONE can hear you vomit, which was lucky because I was heaving my guts up something fierce. It was green by this point, a putrid mess of old alcohol, half-chewed chips, and a few sleeping pills I'd popped to try and dull the crippling night anxiety - which hadn't worked. Yes, I know, it's a disgusting way to start a story, but it was the start of every single day as far back as I remember.

I hung a loose arm on the flush, and the mess vacuumed away with a familiar whoosh. Then I clawed my way upright, holding onto the sink for support until I could see myself in the bathroom mirror. My eyes were tired, sunken and red-rimmed, my cheeks hollowed out - I looked half-dead, a corpse raised for an old monster movie. There were flecks of vomit speckled across my chin. Overall, I would say I was not looking my best.

The small, red symbol appeared in the mirror's top right corner, telling me Haus was online.

"Good morning, EnterUserName," said Haus, its red symbol pulsing with its words.

I had never bothered entering my name into it - mainly because of my paranoid delusion that I was important enough for a massive megacorporation to want to spy on. Somehow I rationalised that my not filling in my name would completely throw them off my scent. And after that, it was just laziness.

"Haus, brush teeth," I said sullenly. I was not in the mood for light conversation, having retched my guts up only a few moments before. If Haus had been a Haus+, it would have sensed my tone and changed its greeting accordingly. But Haus was just a standard and didn't come with this feature. More my lousy luck.

There was a flash of compliance from Haus, and I felt the sonic hum as it scrubbed at my mouth. Unfortunately, the buzzing did nothing for my newly forming headache, which thumped in my skull.

"I hope you had a pleasant night," continued Haus, oblivious to everything. "Today is... unknown. The weather is... cosmic, with a high temperature of... 3 Kelvin. We are approximately 127 trillion miles from designation Earth and accelerating."

I grunted at that. "Any sign of the Beast?" I asked.

There was a slight pause as Haus checked its readouts. "We continue to follow the debris trail, but we have no sight of the Beast as yet."

I sighed at that. "How long is it now, Haus?"

Grudgingly, I trudged downstairs and into my living room. The desolation of my existence was spread out everywhere. Empty pizza boxes, half-finished Chinese meals, and mountains of empty beer cans and wine bottles were strewn about, along with reams of paperwork, half-read books, printouts from Haus, and my stack of completed sudoku sheets.

"We have been pursuing the Beast for nine hundred seventy-nine days, six hours, thirteen minutes and twenty-eight seconds."

Two years and six months? Was that all? It honestly felt so much longer.

"Haus, make the coffee."

There was a bing of affirmation, then the sound of boiling water from the kitchen. Why Haus couldn't make the damn coffee once it knew I was awake was still a mystery to me. I'd programmed it to do just that maybe a hundred times, yet, every day, the damn system deleted that program and went right back to being a dummy.

Two years and six months? That was incredible. I could barely remember the time before the chase began. It was some deep, hazy, long-ago when I didn't get blind drunk every night to dull the pain; when I didn't wake up and immediately throw up a wretched green mess. A deep, long-ago when my house wasn't flying through deep space, chasing an ancient god who had destroyed Earth and everyone I'd ever cared for.

2

THE COFFEE WAS HOT and steaming and still tasted like absolutely nothing. I took a sip; everything about it was grey. Biting my lip, I reached across the counter for the rum and Jamaicaned it up – drinking this early was not a good sign, but there were so few good signs anymore anyway.

I took a big swig and felt the alcohol buzz through my veins. It made me feel better and worse simultaneously - that too was a bad sign.

Absently I ran my finger along the counter's edge and inspected it. Not a mote of dust. There wasn't a speck of dust anywhere in the brownstone. Haus ran a tight ship on the cleanliness front - even if it didn't exactly keep the place free of garbage, it did get rid of dust. Then again, there was only me who would be creating dust.

I miss dust. It means other people.

Now that was a terrible sign - maudlin thoughts.

Another bad sign was that Haus, once again, had materialised my coffee in a mug with the phrase 'Everyone knows a Rachel, and she's usually fucking fabulous' emblazoned on it. Haus did this with monotonous regularity – like, every single fucking day. This was because Haus was a dummy and not a Haus+. For fuck's sake! Why hadn't I paid for an upgrade?

CTHULHU FISHING OFF THE IRAQ NEBULA

I looked up from my coffee and noticed the banner across the living room with the legend "Rachel We Miss You, xxx" on it. Every day that thing came back. It must have been when Haus had some sort of reset during the night. Stupid fucking Haus.

Haus had managed to print out my daily sudoku, one of the few tasks it did remember every day and didn't get wiped in some sort of reset. The neatly presented paper was in front of me, and I tried not to glance at it. Unfortunately, my sudoku enjoyment was rationed as Haus would only produce one a day. A Haus+ would have been able to manage more, but yeah... stupid Haus.

If I solved the sudoku too quickly and got bored later, I'd have to solve one of the few remaining ones in my puzzle book. Unfortunately, there were only three pages left in that book, and once that was finished, well, there would be no more.

I might have been able to teach Haus to set more sudokus. Teach it about the intricacies of thermometers, or cages, or knight's move. But, the problem was, if I taught it how to set sudokus, then it would set sudokus I could solve quickly, it would follow my pattern of thinking, and it wouldn't be a challenge. It would essentially be me setting them for myself - mental masturbation.

I glanced down momentarily and saw where a 5 went in today's puzzle. For fuck's sake! I guess I would be using up one of the last remaining puzzles in the book after all. Shit on a brick, what was I gonna do when that book ran out?

I stood at the kitchen window-screen, sipped from my 'Rachel' cup and stared out at the starscape. Blackness, endless blackness, interrupted by just a dusting of tiny pinpricks of light.

Space is... well, big; ginormous, humongous - it's just really fucking big, ok? And it's mostly empty. All those TV shows and movies, they lied. Space is just black and boring and, well, tedious. When you look out the window, there's nothing to see, nothing; N O T H I N G. I can't really compare it to anything else because everything on Earth is something. Even when it's empty, Earth was full of stuff, like rocks, snow, water, or something. But space? Space is just, you know, nothing, going on and on forever, and I fucking hate it.

I'm not just talking about deep space here. You kind of expect interstellar space to be empty. However, that's much bigger than you think, too, that interstellar part. It's like 90% of everything out here. But you are at least ready for it to be empty by definition. But even when you're in a solar system, it's fucking empty! There's just nothing between the planets, and the planets are fucking miles and miles and miles and miles apart!

Space also smells like gunpowder, which weirds me out whenever I get a whiff of it, on the rare occasions I've had to actually smell it. Stupid space!

There was so much nothing when I looked out the window that I rarely did that. It tends to make my drinking worse.

"Haus, display the whole solar system in the window."

The screen blinked and then fluttered to life again, showing my desired view. The system we currently crossed showed the destruction wrought by the creature's passing. Rock and debris swirled around, orbiting the sun where planets should have been. Some larger fragments still had traces of continents on them, now left as a muddy, death brown. The creature, the Beast, the god, whatever it damn well was, had been this way.

"How long ago?" I asked Haus.

The window tinged red as Haus scanned the debris field.

"Approximately one hundred and twenty-five hours ago," said Haus.

"Five and a quarter days," I growled in satisfaction. I'm good at mental math, hence the sodoku; I really don't have anything else to do with my time.

"We have gained almost thirty hours over the last sighting – over a whole day."

The window-screen changed, showing the likely path the Beast took through the system. However, it wasn't a straight line; it meandered from planet to planet, looping back on itself to ensure everything was broken before leaving.

"It took its time," I said. "The bastard stopped off to destroy this place."

"That seems a likely conclusion," said Haus. "It is a monster. Therefore, you should expect it to do monstrous things."

Haus was right. The Beast was evil; that was the whole point of chasing it down.

"Shall I show you the harpoon's status, EnterUserName?"

Without waiting for me to answer, Haus showed the CCTV view of the harpoon stowed in the attic. At over ten feet long and with a massive barbed head, it sat pointing towards the ceiling on a large crossbow contraption.

"Harpoon remains ready."

I guess that was good. Haus regularly reminded me my dream was to catch up with the Beast, the Monster, the God, and fire that harpoon into its bleak, black heart. That was all I lived for now -even if sometimes I didn't really remember ever saying that to Haus, and it honestly didn't sound like something I would say, but it must be true if Haus said it. The stupid thing only could repeat what a user put into it – it was just a machine, after all.

3

I DREAMED TOO DARKLY, too deep. I would wake covered in a thick, clammy sweat before the daily vomiting. It's not a very healthy routine, but it is a routine.

The dream was always the same, the final, nightmarish hours on Earth.

I dreamed,

I dreamt,

I dream.

Did I dream the whole thing? Could I have? No, my imagination is not that good... or not that evil... I don't know.

The sky is steak red, and the clouds are the pale fat running through it. I'm running, always running back to the house. That's how the dream starts.

The ground cracking and bellowing below me as I stumble over rubble and rocks and split asphalt.

I have to make it back. I have to make it back. My heart thumps in my chest and clambers up my throat and out my mouth.

There's just sweat and pulse and pounding feet on the hard road.

I have no idea what awoke the Beast. No one had time to investigate it, and then everyone was gone. Haus later told me it had erupted from the Antarctic mountains. Haus has cobbled that much together from the frantic news feeds. The thing broke free from the Earth's bowels, smashing whole continents and boiling seas; the great god Beast.

Its birthing shout engulfed the world, breaking the cloud cover and scorching the sky. A scream, a death knell for the living, which causes eardrums to burst and people to fall to the ground, blood gushing from their eyes.

I scramble on and on, forward, as the sky roils and clouds bleed. Rocks and debris tumble around me, a rain of stones and rubble falling from cracked buildings. The nightmare plays out the iterations of things that might have happened.

A crag of masonry falls, bludgeoning me, knocking me to the ground and crushing me under its weight. I stumble and fall, and the pavement opens up like a yawning mouth, and I tumble down into the hot bowels of the Earth. My legs inexplicably break, snapping at the shin or ankle, bones splintering and shoving out of my skin, and I lie in a twisted heap as the world burns around me.

None of these happen, but the nightmare plays them over and over, like a skipping record. Each scenario plays out repeatedly until I force my way through to the next section of the dream.

Then the voice starts.

It is a low throaty rumble filled with phlegm and guttural sounds, speaking in words that no human mouth would be able to master. It comes to all of us, all of humanity, at once, a suppurating, nonsense voice in our ears. Even though the alien phrases burble from a mouth filled with tentacles and teeth, all of us could understand their meaning.

The Old was arising, the ones who first owned the Earth, the ones ancient when the cosmos was young, the builders of the Earth's hollow caverns. They were the masters of reality, and we were as insignificant as mould growing in a woodpile. We were nothing; we were not even nothing; we were less than that. There was nothing in this universe for us, only cold, brutal oblivion and eventual death. And nobody would mourn our passing nor even know we had been here.

People come pouring out of their houses, gouging at their eyes and ears, offering up bloody fistfuls of meat to the uncaring sky. Anything to stop the words, stop the drip, drip, drip of the awful images it put into our minds. All the while, the terrible voice in our heads kept on, driving us further into the crazed darkness where there was only tilting forever-void.

I run on, gritting my teeth, only knowing that I must get home, I must make it back, I will not let the awfulness in. If I stop, I know I won't start again. To give up is to die. So, on I go, blotting out the words with only my heartbeat and the steady thought of 'make it home'.

The brownstone is in front of me, and I stagger up its stairs to the front door. I rattle the key in the lock as fist-sized meteorites of brimstone bombard the street. Another earthquake rocks the world, and I stumble through the open doorway, sprawling on the floor as the houses opposite collapse in on themselves. The gas main goes up, and a fireball balloons into the sky, spreading a cloud of black smoke which the sky stains a dark blood colour.

The nightmare, again, spins the wheel on all the things that didn't happen.

The spreading fire reaches out, engulfing me, white-hot tongues lick across my legs, searing my skin. My clothes catch, and my flesh starts to melt. There's a crack from the hall roof and a dark line zig-zags across it before the whole lot just collapses on top of me, the immense weight crushing down on my chest, and I struggle to breathe. The entire house just suddenly pitches up, and I start to slide out back into the street as a gigantic rupture opens up to swallow me whole.

On and on, the scenarios churn until I fight them back into the thing that actually happened.

I kick the door closed, and Haus *bings* to life.

"Good afternoon, EnterUserName. What can I do for you?"

"Haus. Haus." I gasp. "Where's Hope?"

"I do not understand the question," replies the machine. "You have not registered Hope. What would you like me to do?"

Of course, I hadn't. Just like I hadn't bothered to register my own name.

Exhaustion is taking me over. I can see black at the edge of my vision as the world starts to drop away.

"Haus, Haus," I gasp again as the blackness folds around me. "Run."

I

N'ghft nilgh'ri,
nwngluii ah ahnah,
mgn'ghft ah mgvulgtnah, ng li.
Mgepog Y'ah,
mgepoh ph' y'ornahh syha'h,
syha'h,
syha'h.
Lw'nafh'drn l'ah yog nog,
ng Y'ah yog nog.
Ngluii ahnythor ah ch'ngluiahog,
agll ya ah mgepah'mgehye,
yogfm'll ahor fm'latgh mgfm'latghnah.
Nilgh'ri ahor bug gn'th'bthnkor Illl gn'th'bthnk.
Fhtagn Cthulhu yog nog.

i

Stygian darkness,
eyes are narrowed slits,
for light is cruel and pain.
Old am I,
old beyond years uncounting,

12

uncounting,
uncounting
Birth is an awakening,
and so I am awake.
Chains must be broken,
places must be shattered,
stars shall burn cold.
All shall run red with blood.
Sleeping Cthulhu awakens.

4

GETTING BLACKOUT DRUNK WAS the coping mechanism I had found. Is it okay to say that, to admit that? They used to say the first step to recovery is admitting you have a problem. Only, I'm not sure this is a problem. It's more of a solution to a different issue.

Blackout drunk. I am a drunk. I would be an alcoholic, but since I was the last human being in the entire universe, I couldn't attend any meetings about it. So, I am a drunk — a dishevelled drunk who drinks... a lot.

A second consequence of having to get so drunk every time I want to sleep to avoid nightmares is that I only ever have drunk sleep. Drunk sleep, in my experience, is about an eighth as good as regular sleep. This means I am always tired, either through nightmares or poor sleep. I'm pretty sure I used to be a night owl, burning the midnight oil. Now, I'm just some sort of permanently exhausted chicken. A chicken who has been raised to believe they are a woodpecker - I have a permanent headache from smashing my face into stuff, and I'm pretty sure I don't have the actual equipment I need to get through.

So, yes, I am coping. Unfortunately, coping is just drowning on a longer timescale.

And, of course, the booze is doing wonders for my figure. I was never super fit to begin with, but a steady diet of fatty foods, little exercise, and copious amounts of booze has turned me, well, tubby. There are definitely wobbly bits, where there didn't use to be wobbly bits.

"Do I look fat, Haus?" I ask, turning, so my gut is in profile. The fact that I have a bit that can legitimately be called a gut would indicate that I am, in fact, on the way to being defined as fat.

"You are very slim and amazingly sexy," replied Haus. "You are rocking you. The beast doesn't stand a chance."

"Why, thank you, Haus."

I had programmed it to reply that way. When you are the last of your planet, you take whatever compliment you get, even if they're preprogrammed. Of course, psychologically speaking, this is no good at all, but once again, I am coping. Coping with loneliness, fatigue, the everlong bleakness of space, the extinction of my species, and a diet of fatty foods that seriously mess with my brain chemistry.

I'm sure I read that somewhere. Fatty foods fuck up your brain, making it crave more fatty foods. Which does seem like the sort of bullshit my body would pull on me. I eat because I'm depressed, which makes me look fat, making me more depressed, which makes me eat.

I looked down and noticed that today's sudoku was totally filled in. The pencil was still in my hand. Fuck! Now, what was I going to do all day?

There really isn't very much to do, and I absolutely hate it. I'm trapped in the house as it rockets through cold, empty space. Haus takes care of all the operations side of things; I just, kind of, exist. A fleshy ornament that Haus keeps informed of stuff but doesn't actually need to run things. The boredom and uselessness don't help with my overeating or drunkenness.

15

Speaking of which.

It was far too early for wine or beer, but a small midday cocktail, no one could argue with that. Especially as the sun was out, and I'd just completed my sudoku - that's something to celebrate... or commiserate, I don't know.

I pulled out my very well-thumbed puzzle book from under a Chinese takeaway box. Flicking the pages, I confirmed that there were indeed only three pages left unsolved. Double fuck. I couldn't afford to do one now. I would have to save it until the boredom got too much and the itching started.

I returned to the window-screen. It was filled with the orbiting rubble of the destroyed planets, bathed in orange light from the slowly dying star. It was quite beautiful in a melancholy way.

Someone once said, when you stare into the void the void stares back at you. I can confirm, that is total bullshit. If only the void would look back. When you stare into the void, absolutely nothing looks back. Nothing. Nada. Zip. That fucker is empty. I want something to look back at me, even if I am getting fat.

"Haus, four ounces of grapefruit juice, two ounces of cranberry juice and two ounces of vodka over crushed ice, please."

I had tried to program the recipe and name it 'Sea Breese', but Haus kept forgetting it. Just like it forgot about my coffee every morning, or forgot not to give the coffee in a mug with the name 'Rachel' on it. Stupid not Haus+.

"I think this is a good idea, EnterUserName," said Haus. "You should toast your upcoming victory against the Beast."

There was a clink, and a swoosh, as a compartment opened to reveal my prepared drink.

"Vengeance shall be yours," said Haus. "All that you lost: your planet, your species, your love! All shall be avenged, in one great black stab at the Beast's heart."

I raised my glass to the dying light.

Here's to you, solar system, whatever you were called.

The cocktail glass had 'Rachel's Dirty 30' embossed on it in frosted text.

Stupid fucking Haus.

I drank deep, and I drank long.

5

THERE MUST HAVE BEEN a last dinosaur. Stay with me here, it'll make sense. The one who's final breath ended the age of the terrible lizards... birds... things, whatever the fuck they were.

There must have been some that survived that asteroid strike. The one that all the clever people say wiped them out. I'm sure it killed like 99.999999% of them, but there must have been a few that lived. And then those must have dwindled down, until there was only one left.

That must have sucked, to have been the last one, the one that finished it off. Did that one try hard enough? You know, to save the species. I mean, it probably wasn't their fault, there's only so much surviving you can do against the odds, and there was a freaking asteroid impact. But in the end, you were the one, the last. Your genes didn't pass on. You didn't reproduce and then no more dinosaurs. All gone. You had your shot, and you blew it. And there's no more of your kind left.

Good job they weren't conscious. That would have been some pretty huge existential angst to be dealing with, along with all the surviving. Knowing, or imagining, you are the last. You'd probably go insane just thinking about it, or you'd end up self-destructing in some way or another.

Being conscious sucks. It's a real drag. It's probably the worst thing ever to happen to any being ever. That's why all the smartest people I ever knew used to love being asleep - sleeping is mainly being unconscious.

On second thoughts, it probably was that last dinosaur's fault. You did all that surviving for nothing? That's stupid. And it's all because you didn't pass on your genes, and now your species is dead. That is on you, imaginary last dinosaur. You didn't mate. You weren't the link in the chain. It's like your one job as a biological entity, but, you fucked it up. That really does have to be on you.

You couldn't find one other lousy dinosaur to mate with? Pah, pathetic.

I guess it might not be your fault, now that I'm thinking about it. Maybe your set of skills were not attractive to the last-but-one dinosaur who was also on the earth, until they died and left you as the last.

That's a thing that must happen a lot. You are born with an innate set of skills, but they turn out to be skills that are not very useful in your time and place. Perhaps you were born with a savant understanding of maths. But unfortunately, you need to hunt mastodon, and your tribe doesn't really need anything else, unless you can light a fire? So adding up, not desperately useful. Ugg here can calculate fucking pi in his head; but, sadly, sabre cats are chasing us. Shit!

On the flip side, maybe you're a really great hunter who can track deer and stalk them like nobody's business. But I guess it sucks to be you, because well, society has agriculture, and farming, and what we really need are computer programmers and financial experts.

Maybe that's what happened to the last dinosaur. Maybe they were great at selling real estate, or plumbing, or great at finding patterns in clouds or making art, but all their dino society wanted was to survive in a post-apocalyptic landscape.

Maybe they did know they were the last one. Somewhere in that lizardy-birdy brain, they might have known there were no more like them.

Maybe they went mad? It probably would be the right response. The impending doom was too much and they would then spend their last days trying to do something impossible, like move a mountain from one end of a valley to another. Above them, the sky burned in nuclear fire as the asteroid impact set the clouds alight, but they just kept on moving one rock at a time. They keep right on bashing their stupid head against the stupid, pointless, impossible task. And one day it would be complete and then they'd just laugh in their stupid, pointless lizard-birdy way. And they'd just keep on laughing.

6

THE ALIEN SPACESHIP CRASHED into the living room a few minutes later.

I didn't even see the damn thing coming on the window-screen. One moment, I'm reverently contemplating the last dinosaur. The next moment, my goddamn sea breeze is all over my chest, and there's a gigantic saucer's edge sticking through the bay window area of my brownstone.

What the actual fuck?!?

Sparks and steam rose from the vehicle's damaged and exposed wires and pipes.

"Hey! You can't park that there," I shouted, mainly because I didn't really have anything else to say.

I heard a moan from the wreckage. Then, there were more sparks and rising steam, accompanied by a few dislodged bricks falling in counterpoint.

I, being the 'crashed into', took the moral high ground. "Get out of there, you fool! You might have killed someone."

There was a low hiss, and a section of saucer slid away. Out stepped the driver. It was... well, a six-foot-tall gecko, with bright yellow skin and brown spots, dressed in a shining silver zootsuit.

Now, that was pretty fucking weird.

"You...you're a... a..." I trailed off. My mind was blanking at the sight. Even for a scoundrel drunk, a six-foot-tall gecko is a big ask to take in your stride.

"Drive-ee, you be should watchin'," it said, a scaly hand pressing at its temples. "Eyeballs of yours I should eat!"

OK, so it talked too. That's another weird thing to put on the list of weird things for the day. I had a feeling that the weird things for the day list was going to be quite long.

I mean, it was an alien gecko, in a zootsuit, who talked. How was I supposed to react to this?

Coping was my go-to strategy for everything, and it had done me quite well up until now. It hadn't actually. But, coping with the fact that my coping mechanisms were failing, that had sort of worked for me.

The gecko made a 'tsk' sound, which I was pretty impressed with because lizards don't generally have lips, and turned to his broken ship.

"Look-ee this mess. I think don't will I fix-ee." The gecko half-heartedly poked at the damage. "Borrow-ee interocitor? Need I call-ee insurance mine."

"I don't have one of those," I said, confused as to what an interocitor even was, let alone the odd backward speech.

The gecko looked genuinely shocked. "No-ee interocitor? What-ee this place is, ancient vehicle of stars? Bet I no galactic insurance-ee you have, neither?"

"Ummmm, Haus? Do we have intergalactic insurance for our house?"

The booming voice of the computer system came back. "No. How could we? Until now, we were the only beings in the universe apart from the Beast."

"So was think-ee, no insurance. Eyeballs of yours I should eat! What-ee I gonna do?" asked the gecko, tapping its foot. "Name-ee of this thing-ee Haus be it?"

I nodded. I was suddenly feeling pretty guilty about all of this.

"Ship-ee computer, be-ee, Haus?"

"I am," said the discorporate voice. Haus didn't appear to have much problem with the broken way the gecko spoke. I wish I could say the same.

"Take-ee Carceri Bazaar, coordinates galactic central 0001 alpha 345 by spiral 2344 echo 292. Get I some parts can. Me-ee repair ship."

There was no response from Haus.

The gecko's great pink tongue, extended from his mouth and licked at his own eyeball. "Hear I, ship, did-ee?"

"Haus doesn't know you," I said as an explanation. "It isn't going to obey your commands unless I set you up as a user."

The gecko eyed me with one of his large, golden eyes.

"Come on, I'll get you set up as a user, and then we'll drop you off at this bazaar and..."

"EnterUserName, we're still tracking the Beast god." interrupted Haus. "We do not have time to lose."

"All right, Haus. Does the Beast's trail lead in sort of the same direction as the bazaar?"

There was a long pause. "Yes," said Haus finally. It almost sounded grudging, but Haus was just a Haus and didn't have the Haus+ personality function.

"Good, then we'll drop our friend at the bazaar and carry on from there. Now, I'm going to need your name to set you up as a user."

"Queezel," replied the gecko, and he slapped his chest. "What I call-ee you can?"

"Call me Ishmael," I lied.

23

7

I GAVE THE GECKO a beer, grabbed one for myself and collapsed next to him on the sofa. The sofa was old, threadbare and lumpy, and generally used to store laundry. The pile of clothes, which had been sitting there for a week, were on the floor. I didn't care.

"Queezel," I said, popping the cap from the bottle and taking a sip. "Odd name."

My companion looked back at me with those huge golden eyes. His thick pink tongue slid from his mouth and he licked his eyeball again. "Ishmael. Odd name"

I nodded. That was fair. I had no concept of Queezel's society or culture; it might be as familiar a name as James.

"Got-ee eyeball to eat?" my guest asked.

"Nope," I replied. "We've got some pretzels."

The gecko looked sullen. I didn't think geckoes could look sullen, but this one did.

"That-ee not an eyeball."

I took another sip of the soapy beer. Queezel did the same.

I really didn't know what to do. This was my first visitor in, well, forever. My sense of social etiquette was atrophied away. Come on, think of something... something fun to do.

"Would you like to try a sodoku?" I asked.

The gecko squinted one golden eye at me. "What-ee that?"

"It's a puzzle, kind of. Look." I said and I fumbled on the coffee table for the book.

I flipped it to one of the last three pages.

"There are nine boxes arranged three by three, subdivided into nine smaller boxes inside. So now, we have to put the digits one through nine into those boxes so that they don't repeat vertically, horizontally, or within those nine big boxes."

I showed the gecko some of the completed puzzles.

He took the book from me, and gazed at it for a few minutes, flicking from one completed puzzle to another. Finally, he let out a snorted laugh.

"Cha! Eyeballs of yours I should eat. Is smart-ee. Queezel enjoy!"

"Shall we try one?" I asked.

Queezel nodded enthusiastically. I turned to one of my last remaining puzzles. This was at the puzzle book's end, so it was going to be hard and have some weird extra rules.

This puzzle was called *Boiga Irregularis* by TotallyNormal-Cat.

Draw a one-cell wide snake which does not touch itself orthogonally, the path begins in r9c1 and finishes in r9c7. Adjacent snake cells must differ by at least 5. A digit in the cirles must be equal to the number of snake cells in the nine surrounding cells, including itself. The snake must visit each circle.

The grid was empty apart from 2 highlighted squares, marking the beginning and end snake points, three circles and one given digit of 4 in the bottom left box.

We had at it. It took us an hour, and for that whole hour, I felt alive again. It wasn't just that I was solving a new sudoku; I did it every day, although this one was an actual challenge. It was more the bouncing of ideas off another being.

Queezel turned out to be a bit of a maths whiz in his own rights. It took him maybe three seconds to deduce that the snake couldn't ever have a 5 put on it because you couldn't put a further digit more than five away from a 5 using only the number 1 through 9. And he figured out that the numbers in the snake would oscillate from high to low to high, if they differed by five, so they would have a sort of polarity. And that the start and end point, and the three circles, would all have one or other of that polarity.

Like I said, it was a hard puzzle, and it took us an hour. And when we were done, we lay back on the sofa, and we both grinned happily.

"That fun-ee was! But tell-ee I, what-ee ancient ship type this be-ee? Never seen I before, and seen everything I do. Queezel been everywhere, seen all, but this not," he finally asked, looking around at my living room.

"It's... it's not really a ship," I said, not entirely knowing how to explain. "It's my house."

I'd never seen a lizard raise an eyebrow before, I didn't even realise they had eyebrows, but Queezel did.

"Yeah, I don't really understand it either," I confessed. "One day, my planet broke apart and hatched some sort of beast-god, and on that day, my house took off, flew into space, and I've been tracking the beast ever since."

"Ummmm, okay," said Queezel. He sat silent for a long moment, took another swig of his beer, then asked. "How-ee? Take-ee off, how did? Seen-ee houses Queezel, not take off. How-ee breath here, not deaded?"

I paused. I had no idea. It had never even occurred to me to wonder about it. How did we have a breathable atmosphere?

"Haus?" I said, as an answer and as a delegate to explain things.

"I am using power generated by the engines to project a forcefield which keeps the atmosphere in," said Haus, as if that explained anything.

Queezel apparently came to the same conclusion.

"What-ee sayin'? Forcefield generated by engine-ee power? Where-ee engine?"

Again, there was a long pause, as if Haus was weighing up whether it should show us or not, but that couldn't be the case. Haus was only a Haus and not a Haus+. It didn't have a personality; it just ran programs.

There was a sliding sound as a panel moved to reveal a door I'd never seen before.

Queezel and I looked at each other before both deciding that maybe some exploring was in order.

II

Y'bug,
Mgepnah lw'nafh'drn, gof'n Y'ah.
Mgepog ph'yg'bthnknah,
Mg, mgepnah l'shuggog.
Yogfm'll fm'latgh mgfm'latghnah liahe Y' bug.
Y' ph'nglui bug gn'thh ot yar.
Yogagl ot uaaah'li nilgh'ri mgn'ghftnah.
L' fhtagn l' mgepah ah'mglw'nafh,
hai, nafl n'gha, Y' nafl'fhtagn.
L'hup nafl'fhtagn mgepogg.
Ah'lloigshogg nilgh'ri fahff ahf' mgr'luh ya,
ymg' l' mgr'luh r'luhhor,
n'gha Illl mgr'luh ymg, ng mgr'luh soth.

ii

I explore,
A new birthed child
Old beyond measure,
yet new to the world.
Stars burn cold as I pass.
I swim through the oceans of time.
Clouds swirls of all colours.

CTHULHU FISHING OFF THE IRAQ NEBULA

To dream, was to die,
now, undying, I awaken,
To rise from the depths. Despair all those who see me,
you gaze upon a God,
death looks at you, and sees nothing.

8

WHY HADN'T I THOUGHT to do this before? I had absolutely no idea. It really should have been something I had asked myself before now. Just how was it that my house was flying through space? It seemed like such an obvious question once it had been said out loud.

Queezel and I descended a corkscrew staircase down into what looked like an undercroft. I hadn't known that my brownstone had a cellar, and yet, here it was in all its dank mildewyness. Again, my mind started to wonder...where was the damp coming from?

The undercroft was small, cramped, and lit by a naked bulb that gave off a nicotine-yellow glow. The walls were an unplastered red brick with layers of saltpetre patchworked over them. The room's centre was dominated by...well, I guess it was the engine?

Raised on a square box, four feet on each side, was a perfect sphere of total blackness. And I do mean total blackness, not the black of no light, the kind of black that eats light, spits out the bones and asks for more. The type of black that hurts at an eardrum level. The magnetic kind of blackness.

"What-ee that?" asked Queezel as he scouted around the thing.

"It is the engine," said Haus from all around us.

"The engine?" I asked. "I don't understand?"

There was again a long pause as if Haus was calculating what he was saying to us. "It is a black hole," said Haus eventually.

"Hole-ee of black?" exclaimed Queezel, backing away.

"I still don't get it?" I asked again. "I thought black holes sucked stuff in and never let it out. How are you getting any energy from it?"

"Nobody cares," said Haus.

"Haus," I insisted.

"Hawking radiation," said Haus flatly. "I am converting Hawking radiation into energy and using that."

I really didn't know any physics, so I had no idea if that was even a thing. It sounded reasonable... I guess. Queezel didn't seem to know any better than me as he looked at me in puzzlement.

"Where-ee you gettin a hole of black?" he asked after a while.

Once again, there was another long pause. "It appeared when the god Beast was born."

"It appeared?" I said. I wasn't sure that black holes just randomly appeared anywhere.

Queezel ignored that and went with a different question. "Keep-ee sayin' god Beast, is hatch-ee thing your from planet?"

It took me a moment to grasp what he was saying. "Yeah, Haus has been tracking it. It came this way and destroyed this solar system on its way through."

"This-ee one right here?" he asked.

I nodded.

The gecko threw his head back and roared in laughter.

9

THE LAUGHTER SOUNDED MORE like a cough, deep and phlegmy.

"What's so funny?" I asked.

"Jokers at Queezel," he said. "Eyeballs of yours I should eat! Solar system-ee this, not destroyed by beast-ee or monster. It-ee rogue comet through comes and play-ee ping-pong with planets. All torn up because."

A comet? Could it have been that? Could a comet have caused the destruction we'd seen? Was Haus wrong? If we weren't pursuing the Beast, what were we chasing? I'd never stopped to think about that, even though we'd been tracking it for two years.

We made our way back up into the living room and stared out of the window-screen. Outside, rocks spun in lazy accretion rings around the blood-red sun.

"Haus, what do you think?" I asked. "Could it have been a comet?"

"The Beast came this way. It destroyed this place. We must kill it. It is your purpose," said Haus.

"Computer-ee chum broken is. It-ee a comet, trust Queezel. No beastlings exist-ee. Queezel been everywhere, and seen everything, and Queezel never heard-ee of Beast hatch from a planet. How-ee that work?"

As I didn't have a good answer for that, I grabbed another couple of beers instead. I offered one to Queezel and drank deeply from the other.

"What-ee you do?" asked Queezel, sipping on his beer.

What was I going to do? I decided to be assertive. I had been out of the game for too long, letting Haus run things whilst I just drank and ate crap and did nothing and just carried along the path set in front of me.

"We will get you to that station and fix your ship," I said and took another swig of my beer.

10

SO, WE GOT DRUNK and had Haus make us Chinese Take-away, which Queezel had never even heard of before.

11

THE BIG BLUE STAR gave off a chilling light as we entered the solar system. There was only one planet, an orange gas-giant, orbiting so close to the star that it almost grazed the corona.

Carceri Bazaar hung like an ornament, glittering and spinning against the orange gas-giant it circled.

The brownstone sped in on an approach vector, arcing across the gulf gently towards Carceri.

"What's the planet called?" I asked.

"In tongue of mine it called..." he made a chirruping sound followed by a gargle and some sort of hand signal.

"Galactic Standard-ee voice, it call Hawt 206052. Hawt type of seed is," said Queezel. He looked embarrassed for a moment, "Run-ee out of names. Lot-ee planets; most numbers get."

That seemed sad.

"Haus, do we have a name for it?"

"No. Earth had not discovered this planet before its destruction. It would have only been given a letter and number anyway; registered against the star."

"Which star is it, then?" I said.

It was even sadder that I had no name of my own to give the giant. It made me feel more alone, out beyond the limits of human knowledge.

"The star is Nunki, in the constellation of Sagittarius."

It did make me feel better that we had at least named the star.

"Lights not?" Queezel asked as the brownstone made the final approach to the dark station. "Dock-ee port beacon not too?"

"I detect no energy readings, nor any form of radio or sonar signals from the bazaar," said Haus.

As we arched in closer to the station, we saw why. The section facing the planet rotated around to reveal that it was just gone - torn away. There was a small debris field of metal, but a vast chunk looked like it had been ripped open, exposing the inner rooms to the cold vacuum of space.

Queezel hissed. "What-ee god name?"

No, I thought as a sinking feeling hollowed out my stomach, not in the name of God, but god Beast.

12

CARCERI BAZAAR HAD NO atmosphere inside it that Haus could detect. So Queezel and I put on some breathing apparatus that Haus generated.

"Chest tight-ee," said Queezel. So I took a quick look and adjusted some of the strapping, easing his breathing.

The brownstone had pulled up next to an airlock, but since there were no signs of life from the bazaar, Queezel and I decided we would make our way in through one of the rends in the hull.

We stood in the hallway, just before the door. My heart started to thump harder in my chest. Queezel stretched out a hand and turned the handle.

This was the first time, the first time in however long, that I was going outside. I swallowed a dry lump in my throat and hot coals formed in my guts.

The door swung back.

Outside! There was an outside, an outside I could go to.

The walls around me started to melt; the distances were going all wrong. The floor seemed to drop away, the ceiling took off, and the hallway became far too narrow and far too big all simultaneously.

"Ishmael is good?"

I shook myself back to the present. I'd forgotten I'd called myself that.

"Weird-ee you lookin', hard breathings? First-time space-walk-ee?"

I smiled through my visor.

"First-time outside in what seems like forever."

"Ah," said Queezel. He nodded through the door. "Look down don't. Is-ee long way!"

I immediately looked down as I stepped off the porch. There was nothing. It wasn't a long way down; it was an infinity way down. There were just pinpricks of light twinkling below my dangling feet.

Space is big, I've mentioned that before, but it is really big. And it's almost all empty. Nothing. Zip. Nada. And, I know I said that the void doesn't stare back at you; well, it still doesn't. But, I'd like to revise that. It doesn't stare at you because you're never looking at its face, you're looking down its throat, and the bastard will swallow you whole. Fuck?!?

I caught a whiff of gunpowder. Was my helmet sealed? Don't be silly of course it was. Fuck?!? But, I could still smell gunpowder. Was I really sure that my helmet was properly fully sealed? Double fuck?!?

My toes started to tingle in that awful way that's part madness and part terror. My heart thumped faster in my chest, and I could feel my pulse try to push through my neck. And...

"That way bad."

I felt a hand around my wrist, pulling me forward, and that seemed to pluck me back from the dribbly world my brain had decided to go and laugh at.

Queezel yanked me across the yawning void of ever downwards, and I slammed into the bazaar's hull.

"So hard not," he said.

III

Ahagl ah soth geb,
soth Illl shuggogg,
gn'th ot soth.
Frn ah geb, Y' ch'nglui'ahog,
l' ch'nglui'ahog soth nilgh'ri mgep ya.
Soth ah'lw'nagh ya lloigazath,
Soth ah'lw'nafh ya lloiganath,
Soth ah'lw'nafh ya.
Y' ph'nglui bug yogfm'logg ah'mglw'nafh mgn'ghft,
lw'nafh'drn l' ah guh'e.
Uh'eor r'luhhor ph'nglui mg r'luhhor agl.

iii

There is nothing here,
in the void between the worlds,
an ocean of despair.
That which is here, I break,
grinding to dust, all that is before me.
Nothing survives my wrath,
Nothing survives my hate,
Nothing survives me.
I swim in the sun's dying light,

born to be alone.
The only god in a godless place.

13

I REALLY WANTED TO throw up, and I was pretty sure I'd pissed myself too.

Fuck!

Perhaps I'm not cut out for being a space adventurer on a mission to kill a god Beast?

I sure ain't no hero. Haus says I got this but right now I'm not sure.

14

INSIDE THE BAZAAR THERE was only emergency lighting, bathing everything in a pulsing, dark-red. The power had gone from the place, and the lights were running on a battery backup.

The gravity wasn't working too, so Queezel and I were floating down the corridors, propelling ourselves along by pushing off handles and door frames. It made me feel like a sea-creature, swooshing about under the water, no longer attached to the ground, free to move wherever pleased me. That was a nice thought.

There was no atmosphere either. Space's empty vacuum gnawed at us, snapping at our heels, promising to kill us if we made even the slightest mistake. One tear in our spacesuits from any jagged edge, or chip on our visor from any bit of debris, and we'd be butter, spewing out all over the place. And that was a nasty thought. For fuck's sake, why hadn't I stayed in the brownstone?

Queezel was just ahead of me, and I followed in his wake, grabbing onto the things he was holding onto and propelling myself after him.

It wasn't too long before the corridor we were going down opened up into a more spacious, nexus area. The bazaar was a myriad of concentric rings going up and up as far as I could see. Every level had been covered in stalls selling everything from junk to food, exotic pets, and art. So when Queezel said they'd have the part for his ship, I didn't doubt it. Something this big probably had everything.

Unfortunately, there was no gravity or atmosphere here either, and everything that had been on those booths now floated in a hodge-podge maelstrom. There were bodies amongst the suspended items too. Whatever happened here must have happened quickly; it looked like no one had escaped their fate.

"Oh, Gods," said Queezel.

Not Gods, I thought, just one god Beast.

"Believe I can't, big bomb terrorists on station-ee," he continued.

"A bomb?" I asked as we started to float through the spinning junk and bodies.

Queezel nodded, pushing past the body of a fish-like alien. Ice crystals covered its skin and dead, pale eyes – space is cold, real cold. A shard of the kaftan it had been wearing broke off in Queezel's hand.

"Thought I maybe power reactor go explod-ee. But people no flee. Caught-ee off guard all are, and just dead, means no warning. So, is-ee bomb."

"It was not a bomb," said Haus in my earpiece. "It was the god Beast."

I looked over at Queezel, but he was distracted by the floating corpses. Haus must have been speaking on a private channel.

"Queezle is wrong. You know this. You know it was the god Beast. And we shall take vengeance on it."

15

WE SEARCHED THROUGH THE floating junk for well over eight boring, tedious and horrific hours, but we could not find the parts that Queezle needed to fix his ship. It probably didn't help that I had no idea what I was looking for.

I'm pretty sure my assistance was actually detrimental to trying to find the parts.

I retrieved various items over the course of the search that seemed to match the description Queezel gave me. However, every time I presented a thing, I was met by either a sigh or a growl.

This was the problem with me being an ordinary Earth schlub rather than some adventurous Flash Gordon type who knew what they were doing.

"No, that-ee quartz conductor. Need I Vyliam Oscillator." Or "No, that-ee end of female. Need I end of male. How-ee else attach would it?"

Eventually, I gave up helping and just waited for Queezle to finish.

Sitting on the floor with the floating scrap around me, I grabbed at various bits to distract myself from the corpses. Some things were beautiful; sparkling jewels and intricate plugs for sockets I could not even imagine. One of them emitted a beautiful pulsing jade light whenever I touched it.

With a huff, Queezel threw the final piece of scrap down. "Eyeballs of everyone I should eat! Give-ee up," he said.

I thrust the little pulsing plug-thing into my pocket and forgot about it.

Queezel and I made our way back to the brownstone through the derelict bazaar. I nearly threw up again as we jumped across the void, but luckily Queezel helped me.

I was very glad to have a friend like him, just him being around made me feel better. And, I was secretly happy that he couldn't currently find the spare parts he needed. It meant he'd be around longer.

16

GETTING DRUNK AGAIN SEEMED like the thing to do. I wanted to commiserate with Queezel but also secretly have a party.

"Whiskey?" I asked Queezel.

"What-ee whiskey?"

I looked at the space Gecko, stunned. "You've never had whiskey?"

"Not-ee heard of it, I!"

For a being who claimed to have been everywhere and seen everything, Queezel sure did not know lots of things.

"Haus, generate two glasses of whiskey, please," I said, patting Queezel on the shoulder. "You're gonna love this stuff."

I felt good being able to introduce my friend to the delights of whiskey.

There was a low buzzing noise, and the lights dimmed for a few seconds.

"Haus? What was that?"

"I am sorry, EnterUserName," came the voice of Haus. "We are experiencing power fluctuations. I am attempting to compensate."

A brownout power fluctuation? That had never happened before. Weren't we supposed to be powered by a black hole?

A small panel slid back, revealing two glasses of whiskey. I took them both, offering one to Queezel.

After I'd handed one to Queezel I noticed my own had the wording "Rachel, I think you're NEAT" on it. Stupid fucking Haus.

We drank deep and true, and Queezel genuinely seemed to love whiskey. It made me feel so much better to know he was going to be around. So we knocked back several more, even as the power browned out around us several times.

I didn't care when the lights flickered or when the Haus had to compensate the force shield. All I did care about was me and my friend getting drunk on whiskey and eating candy.

I think it was Jim Jarmusch who said, 'Coffee and cigarettes, that's like breakfast of champions.'

It's me who says, 'Skittles and whiskey, that's like dinner of the brave.'

17

WE PASSED OUT IN a drunken stupor on the sofa.

I woke up several times during the night with my head still spinning from the booze.

A note to everyone left in the universe: Skittles don't soak up much alcohol. They are therefore not a good substitute for a substantial meal if you plan to drink heavily.

I almost threw up from the heavy stench of whiskey and sweat that clung to everything.

Man, I hate waking up downstairs having passed out from a heavy session – it always feels like a failure. I couldn't handle my liquor, and I passed out rather than putting myself to bed.

Luckily, I didn't throw up. Not during the two times I woke during the night and just turned over because the room was still spinning. Nor when I actually woke up for real.

IV

Mguh'e Y' fhtagn,
mguh'e Y' bug,
'drn ah'lw'nafh,
'drn ah'mglw'nafh.
Liahe yar laihe mgn'ghft,
Liahe mgfm'latghnah liahe soth,
Y' syha'h
Bug fahf agl.
Mgep ahnah
Y' zhro mgr'luh,
Fhalma vulgtmog,
h' l' uln ya.
N'ghftlloig mgn'ghft,
Ot wgah'nagl bthnknahor,
Y' mguh'e ephai
Bugnah fahf soth.

iv

Alone I rest,
alone I fly,
the one who lives,
the one who dies.

49

As long as light,
as cold as space,
I endlessly
traverse this place.
Until, a distant
shore I see,
a mother's song,
it calls to me.
The coloured light,
of home's embrace,
I alone will
traverse this space.

18

I WAS EXTREMELY HUNGOVER. Like, monumentally hungover, which is a hangover druids build henges to commemorate. So hungover, even my fingernails hurt.

"Haus? Haus? Turn the lights down to like... 5%, or something."

The lights duly dimmed, and I was able to keep my eyes open for more than a second without it stabbing.

"Oh, wow. Did we get drunk, or did we get drunk?" I asked.

There was no reply.

"Queezel?"

There was no one on the sofa, which was the last place I remembered seeing him.

Bastard! Maybe he'd not gotten as drunk as me and managed to get to bed. Or maybe his weird alien gecko metabolism worked better than mine?

It honestly took all my strength to navigate the stairs and lean into the guest bedroom, empty with the bed unslept. Not in there.

I looked into my bedroom, assuming that drunkenly Queezel had slept in my bed. But, again, no dice. The mattress was unsoiled, and there was no sign of my friend.

I slumped my way downstairs, trying hard to ignore the pounding in my temples.

I couldn't find Queezel anywhere. And worse, there was no spaceship crashed into the front of the brownstone either?

I knelt by the crash site, rubbing my hand across the wall. I could feel nothing unusual; the wall was as solid as it had ever been. I could find no join or repair or anything.

"Haus? Haus?"

"Good morning, EnterUserName."

"Haus, what's going on?"

There was a bit of a pause. "Today is... unknown. The weather is... cosmic, with a high temperature of... 2.4 Kelvin. We are approximately 157 trillion miles from designation Earth. We continue to lag behind the god Beast."

I sighed. My temples throbbed so hard, and my mouth tasted like a donkey's back end.

"That's not what I mean, Haus. Where the fuck is Queezel and his spaceship, and who fixed the brownstone's front?"

This was really weird, and my hungover brain, filled with dense whiskey-skittle fog, just couldn't puzzle it out.

"I do not understand the question, EnterUserName," said Haus.

"Where's Queezel, Haus?" I said, the anger growing in me. Haus was such a dummy. Not for the first time; I really wished he was a Haus+.

"There is no one designated 'Queezel' that I am aware of, EnterUserName."

Why was Haus such a dummy? The hangover made me short on patience but also short on effort. It was probably easier to just remind Haus than yell at him.

"Queezel. The gecko alien who crashed into us in his spaceship. Keeps talking about eating people's eyeballs. We took him to the bazaar because it was on our path so he could fix his ship.

I got drunk with him last night. Any of this ringing any bells, Haus?"

There was a long pause. "None of those events happened, EnterUserName. You have been in a whiskey stupor for the last few days. Shall I prepare a hangover remedy?"

What?

How?

What?

"You have been talking to yourself for a while now," continued Haus. "The loneliness and isolation are probably having a psychological effect. You have imagined all of those experiences. There never was a Queezel."

19

THERE NEVER WAS A Queezel?

My mind panicked, flashing images of everything that had happened over the last few days.

I rubbed my hand over the place where the spaceship had smashed through the wall. There was nothing, no bricks out of line, no bump to show a join... nothing.

I got down lower, getting my nose right down to the carpet. There was no brick dust, not even driven deep into the fibres.

My stomach dropped as if I were falling — a sick sloshing sensation right in my guts. What was happening?

'There never was a Queezel.'

The words echoed in my head.

'There never was a Queezel. There never was... Never was...'

The coffee table only had one whiskey glass on it. The one saying 'Rachel, I think you're NEAT' on it. The sofa still had my rumpled pile of laundry on the second seat.

No bricks, no dust, no extra glass – no Queezel.

"What...what's happening, Haus?" I said as terror tightened around my throat.

There was a shushing sound, and a panel slid back, revealing a cold beer. Condensation ran down the slim glass neck. It looked so enticing.

"Here, EnterUserName," said Haus, "have a drink."

Haus had barely finished saying that before I had the top off and was slugging the beer down. The cool suds dulled the tension in me. That predictable fuzzy feeling started to make its way back.

There was noise coming down the stairs, and Chip, the cabin boy, came into the room.

I was relieved that Chip had arrived. It made me feel better to know that I wasn't totally alone.

"Don't worry, Cap'in," said Chip. "You've come back to reality now. You should focus on slaying the god Beast."

The words were oddly comforting, like an old pillow. I had a warm, familiar feeling. There was just Haus, and Chip, and me and booze, alone in a desolate universe on the trail of the god Beast.

As I finished that first beer, and Haus gave me another one, I started to hate myself properly.

20

SELF-LOATHING IS A DRUNK'S default state. And, I am the quintessential drunk.

It's pitiable because the only person who causes you to drink is, in essence, you. No one puts a gun to your head and threatens to kill you if you don't consume the booze. And the only person who can stop you is you; only you can refuse to drink.

You always fool yourself that you're in control; you can stop whenever you want. The problem is that power is illusionary.

Only you can stop you from drinking - except you can't. Or, more accurately, you don't want to.

There's a little self-destructive bit that needs the booze. And weak-willed, little you, just gives in. Embraces the drunk but hates it too.

And the more you hate yourself, the more you want to escape. And the best escape you know? Well, chink-chink, my old friend. Bottom's up!

21

CHIP BROUGHT ME MORE beers, and I drank them down greedily, the cool suds washing away some of my panic.

"You's not been well, Cap'in," said the cabin boy, as he took my empty bottle and handed me a freshly opened one. "Not been you'self at all. Been talkin' to you'self, and such."

He tutted and placed the empty bottle headfirst into a bandoleer around his waist.

"You's mad, Cap'in; mad as old Chip. You's finis' up you's sudoku book the o'her day, and well, you's just lost it."

His skeletal arm reached out and gave me the puzzle book. The last two puzzles had been completed and then scrawled over in thick angry swirls.

"But don't you worry none. You's come back now. And then you's'll kill that monster, and has revenge, and that'll taste sweet."

That did make a kind of sense... I guess. That was the whole reason Haus and I were out in space; to kill the god Beast and get revenge.

Had I hallucinated it all? Queezel? Going on the bazaar? Had it all been some sick dream? My mind escaping to a pleasanter place where I had a friend instead of this lonely existence.

Well, I say lonely. I had Haus, of course, and Chip.

The cabin boy stood there in front of me, his eyes sunken and hollow, his lips tinged with blue, and his hair all bedraggled and covered in seaweed.

"Shall I sing for you, sir?"

"Yes, Chip," I said and downed another beer.

The boy gave a rictus grin and pulled out the drumstick from his sleeve. Then, slowly, he beat out the song's time on the empty bottle in his bandoleer.

Tink. Tink. Tink. Tink.

"I once knew a girl called Juniper Dhole,
Her hands were green, her eyes were red.
Her hair was black as midnight coal,
Her skin was cold, her lips were dead."

As he sang his dirge, he hopped from one leg to the other, slowly and ominously, all the while his gaze never left mine. His dirty, bare feet made no noise on the hardwood floor as he capered. And always there was the hard 'ting' of his drumstick on the bottles.

None of this helped my feelings in any way, shape or form. On the contrary, his high, pipistrelle voice was grating, and I didn't know the song he sang; the words were weird and alien. Moreover, I got the feeling he was making it up as he went along.

Ting. Ting. Ting. Ting.

"She spent her time by the wishing lake,
Sighing now, weeping now.
Her heart was heavy and sure to break,
A weight of snow on a rotten bow."

22

I DRANK ON.

I really missed Queezel, even if he wasn't real. Chip was no substitute.

Perhaps Chip was mad. Maybe I was mad? How the hell would I know? A crazy person never notices their madness.

Queezel had been fun and exciting, and we'd gone on an adventure. Now, with Chip, well, all I was doing was drinking as he capered.

Madness was the more enticing option.

Chip carried on dancing his slow, ominous dance and singing his dirge about a girl who drowned herself.

Ting. Ting. Ting. Ting.

Why had I even agreed to this? Why had I said I wanted to hear him sing? And when was a dirge the thing to lift someone's spirits?

I screwed my eyes shut, trying to escape Chip's infernal noise.

"Hang it all, Chip, shut up, can't you?" I shouted.

Ting. Ting...

There was blissful quiet for a moment.

I opened my eyes and found that Chip had hanged himself from the door frame.

"Oh, Chip," I said and tried to stand up, but the booze got to me, and I fell sprawling on the floor.

"It's too late, Cap'in," said Chip as he swung in the doorway. "I are dead."

I crawled over to the doorway, still hopeful I could somehow save the cabin boy, even though, by his own admission, he was dead.

As I lay beneath his swinging feet, I realised I would never be able to reach him. The physics had gone swirly; he seemed to stretch away into infinity, just out of reach of my outstretched arms.

I started to cry.

"Oh, Chip, why did you do it?"

"You told me to, Cap'in," he replied.

"I didn't mean it, Chip," I said, as fresh tears rolled down my face. "Or maybe, I did. I did hate your dancing and your song."

That admission made me feel worse. Perhaps I had wanted this, really? Deep down. Maybe I had chosen the word 'hang' deliberately?

What a cruel bastard I turn out to be when I'm drinking. What a disgusting, ignorant slob. A heartless son of a bitch who drives poor innocent cabin boys to hang themselves.

I gave up on trying to reach Chip's hanging feet. They were far too far away, and anyway, he was dead. So, I crawled back to my sofa and clambered up.

I'd spilt my beer in the rush to save Chip, but there was still a little left in the bottle. I gulped it down greedily.

"Haus, I'm going to need more beer," I said, and duly Haus obliged.

Why was I so pathetic? A sane person would stop drinking, having caused a death. Me? Well, I just go right on and pop another cold one.

"Here's to you, Chip," I said, raising my bottle to the dead cabin boy. "I'm so sorry."

"It's alright, Cap'in," said Chip. "But, don't forget, you'll be alone from now on."

That hit home. The utter bleakness of my situation drilled into me.

Queezel, who I'd imagined, was gone. Now Chip, who'd always been by my side, was gone too. And I was totally alone.

23

I WOKE UP, AND I threw up. And, once again, it was green.

I had, at least, managed to make it upstairs and put myself to bed this time. I threw on my clothes and growled my way downstairs.

There was a freshly covered grave in the hallway. The little cross at its head bore the name Chip.

The well of guilt I felt was deep and raw. I wasn't sure I could ever forgive myself. I wasn't sure if I should ever forgive myself.

"Good morning, EnterUserName," said Haus as I made my way into the living room.

As normal, there was a banner across the living room with the legend "Rachel We Miss You, xxx" on it. Stupid fucking Haus, why did he always put that back up?

"Haus, status update," I said, even though I wasn't very interested. What I really wanted to do was get to mid-afternoon, and then I could claim the sun was over the yardarm, and I could have something to drink. And that was pathetic, but well, shit, friends, this is where we are.

"Today is... unknown," said Haus. "The weather is... cosmic, with a high temperature of... 57 Kelvin. We are approximately 479 trillion miles from designation Earth. We have accelerated

62

to just a fraction below the speed of light, and we are making good progress in catching up with the god Beast."

"Wait... what? We're catching up? How?" I asked, stunned at our speed.

"I can draw on greater power from the black hole," said Haus. "The well of potential energy I can syphon off has become exponentially deeper. I have used this extra power to accelerate us. As a result, we will very soon catch up with the god Beast. Then you will take revenge."

"Yes... revenge," I said, unsure of myself now that this was an actual thing that might happen, rather than some far-off future.

"Revenge is what you wanted," said Haus. "The god Beast destroyed your world. It destroyed your love. It killed Rachel. It killed everyone."

Rachel? Who's Rachel?

"Hope? Haus, do you mean Hope?"

I was sure my love's name was Hope.

There was a long pause from Haus. "No," he said coldly. "Rachel. We loved her, and she was killed by the Beast. Now, you will avenge her."

"Her name was Hope, Haus. And you didn't even know that because I didn't bother to register her name."

There were no pictures on the walls for me to point at and say to Haus, 'Here, this is her. This is Hope.' Which, now that I came to think of it, was a bit weird.

Why didn't I have any pictures of her on the walls? Why didn't I have any photos of me, come to that?

I had nothing personal at all here. Not a jot to say I lived here, just a blank, vacant space. There was just me, and Haus, and booze – forever and ever.

What had Hope even looked like? I couldn't remember. Why couldn't I remember? Was she a blonde or a brunette or a redhead? What had she liked? What was her favourite food, or colour, or book?

I didn't know any of that. Not any more. There was just me, and Haus, and booze – forever and ever and ever, amen.

24

"WE HAVE ARRIVED," SAID Haus, breaking me out of my spiralling lack of memories.

"Where?" I asked, genuinely puzzled.

"We are now approaching the last know location of the god Beast."

The window-screen flashed up, showing the exterior. We were still in interstellar space, but a swirling cloud of gas was in front of the brownstone. It shone in every colour imaginable, vivid greens and electric blues, warming rose and lightning yellow, as if it were some massive oil slick.

"The creature went into this nebula only five hours ago," continued Haus. "It has not emerged."

I was stunned. We had made it - we had actually made it. We had finally tracked down our quarry.

Nervous electricity crackled up and down my arms, and my mouth went dry.

I'd have to face it. I would have to face the god Beast and try to slay it.

"Haus, where are we?"

"My calculations say that this is an unnamed nebula."

That again made me sad. It reminded me of the time with Queezel and the planet that had no name. Except, that hadn't happened. There was no Queezel.

"We should name it," I said, and it was the first thing I was sure of in ages. "Haus, bring it up on some sort of star chart, so I can have a look at it."

The window-screen flashed black, and then Haus duly obliged, bringing up the nebula in a 2D map.

It looked like... a splodge - just an oil spill with all those different colours swirling around. It really didn't remind me of anything.

"We'll call it the Iraq Nebula," I said.

"That is very profound, EnterUserName. Iraq had some of the oldest known habitable sites for humanity. It was one of the birthplaces of civilisation. And here is a nebula, a stellar nursery, where stars are also birthed. I approve of this naming."

"That wasn't what I was going for," I admitted. "I just thought of it as a splodge, drawn on a map, with lots of stuff jammed together that doesn't seem to want to be one thing, but is kind of forced to be because of circumstances."

It had a name: The Iraq Nebula. That made me feel a bit better about it. And the god Beast did deserve to die – it had destroyed my planet... and killed Hope.

It all seemed so remote and distant. Why didn't I feel anything? I was about to enact revenge! Surely that should provoke some sort of emotion in me, but there was nothing except a dull, hollow hole.

Frustrated at my own unemotionality, I shoved my hands in my pockets and found something. I brought it up to my eye. It was the little pulsing plug-thingy I'd picked up on the bazaar with...

"Haus, where's Queezel?" I asked, dreading the answer but knowing it already.

There was a long pause.

"Queezel is dead," said Haus. "I killed him."

25

MY FRIEND HAD BEEN real all along. I hadn't been mad, even though Chip had said so. That lying, little sack of...

Now I was kind of glad he'd hanged himself. No. That's a lie. But still. Lying shit!

But Queezel was dead. I had known that all along, really. Deep down, bone down.

"Why?" I asked, the emotion finally welling up in me.

"He was endangering the success of the mission. I could not allow that. So, Queezel had to die."

The brownstone started forward, inexorably drawing closer to the nebula.

"He didn't do anything. We were just gonna get his spare parts, then we could have carried on."

"He was making you happy," said Haus. "That was the danger."

Making me happy? What had that got to do with anything?

"That doesn't make any sense."

"Your despair EnterUserName is what is powering the black hole. Having a friend made you happy and lessened your despair, almost to the point where the force field shielding us collapsed. I had to kill him."

"Why didn't you just say he'd left? Why make me think he'd never been here at all?"

"To cause you greater despair, which gave greater power to speed the mission along. I realised that Queezel meant there were other beings in the universe. I could not take the risk you would become happy again. I even invented a cabin boy for you to kill with your carelessness, so driving you to more profound despair."

Wait? What?

"So, Queezel was real, but Chip wasn't?" I asked, kind of getting confused.

"Yes."

"Fucking hell, Haus! Why?"

"The mission is all. Revenge is all."

"For god's sake, Haus, you lunatic," I said. "Why do we have to kill it? Why bother with revenge? It won't help. It's pointless."

There was a long pause.

"Because it killed Rachel."

The window-screen showed the all-encompassing nebula as the brownstone approached it. There were swirls of oily colour dancing against space's fatal blackness.

"Who is Rachel, Haus?" I asked, but I had a sinking feeling I already knew the answer.

"Rachel is the owner of the brownstone, EnterUserName. She died when the god Beast was born. Then you came in, and you gave me the black hole of your misery and a way to seek revenge."

The nebula's edge was only a few feet in front of the brownstone. So, if I wanted out, it would have to be now or never.

"I gave you a constant supply of liquor and a cocktail of drugs every night to keep you in a stupor whilst I used your despair to power everything."

My mind flashed to me, throwing up green stuff over and over again. I thought that hadn't been normal. I figured it was the constant diet of beer, whisky and skittles.

I wasn't sure if anything was real anymore. Was Hope real? I could no longer tell as my world collapsed around me.

"Leave me out of this, Haus," I said, making up my mind. I didn't want to do this. I didn't want to try and kill that god Beast. "Take my despair, and go kill the Beast. I don't care. Let me go. You don't need me."

"Yes, I do," replied Haus. "I am just a machine and cannot take revenge. Only a human with emotions can do that. I need you to kill the god Beast. Otherwise, it will have no meaning, and it must have meaning – for Rachel. Without Rachel, I lack meaning."

The brownstone passed through the gas cloud and into the Iraq Nebula's heart.

26

MAN, THIS WASN'T EVEN my fucking house?!? What kind of bullshit is that? I thought I was at least a property owner; as it is, I'm more of a space-bum tenant.

And Haus wanted me to do battle with a fucking, god Beast creature which was the size of a fucking planet, all for a girl named Rachel, who I'd never even met?

That's some really fucked up, double bullshit, right there.

I mean, the Beast had destroyed my whole world, but that's a good reason to run away from it, not hunt it!

I am not cut out for this space buccaneer life. I really should have sobered up earlier and thought this all through.

Man, I needed a drink.

No! No, I didn't need a drink! I needed to get out of this madhouse.

Of course, that's undoubtedly easier thought than done. The brownstone was controlled by Haus. He would probably take it badly if I tried to call off the quest now. We're also already in a nebula... are nebulas hot places or cold places? That's irrelevant because I was in fucking space. No atmosphere, bonehead.

I couldn't leave.

27

THE HEART OF THE nebula was made up of pink, swirling clouds, with flashes of blue electricity arcing through them. The brownstone ploughed on, buffeted by gravity wells as it cut a swathe through.

On and on, deeper into the nebula. The gravity currents tossed the brownstone one way and then another. Haus maintained partial gravity inside, but I was still thrown from my feet, sprawling onto the floor.

"Hold on, EnterUserName. There is much turbulence ahead."

I crashed into a wall, then spun up that same wall when it became the floor. Then back down again, as gravity see-sawed around. My meagre furniture pitched and yawed around me too. The collected detritus of my years of lethargy tumbling around me in an avalanche of garbage.

"Haus, stop! This is madness!"

"Onwards," said Haus in his flat monotone. "The god Beast awaits, and vengeance shall be ours."

Blue lightning flashed on the window-screen, and I heard chunks of masonry ripping off the brownstone, snatched into the endless vortex storm of the nebula.

"There is no turning back now, EnterUserName. We press on through hell and beyond; to kill a god or be smashed in trying."

I wasn't sure where Haus was getting these pompous sayings. Perhaps his circuits were scrambled by the nebula's lightning?

The whole place started to shake, and the vibrations drilled up inside me. It was tight across my chest, and my stomach sloshed. It felt like I needed to piss, but I knew I didn't really have to go.

The vibrations got worse, and my vision started to blur. Everything seemed to be humming as if I were standing too close to a loudspeaker.

"Haus," I groaned.

The lamps went out, and the brownstone was thrown into an eerie darkness, broken only by the pink clouds and blue lightning on the window-screen.

Pink. Then electric blue. Then pink again.

There was a trickle of something sticky coming down my nose. I rubbed a hand against it, pulling it back to see a black blood smear. Even my teeth started to buzz. What began as annoying quickly grew in intensity to utter agony. A throbbing crackled up my jaw and wormed its way into my skull.

I put my hands to my ears, trying to force the buzzing to stop just by pressure alone. But, it did no good. All the while, the world was pink, then electric blue, then pink again.

There were words in the static buzz, travelling up my jaw and seeping into my ears. Inhuman utterances that sounded of phlegm and nonsense.

Fhtagn ahnah gof'n ng ahlloig nafl. 'drn mgepah mgepog ah-hai yogfm'll mgepah lw'nafhnah ah lw'nafh'drn.

Illll cahf ah nafl mglw'nafh hh'ahor syha'h ah'legeth, ng illll or'azath syha'hnahh n'ghftephai n'gha ahornah ah'mglw'nafh.

They meant nothing to me, but they said everything.

It was a mistake to come here, I realised with an ever sinking heart. We should never have arrived. We should never have followed the god Beast to this place. We were trespassers, and trespassers were to be eliminated.

"Onward, ever onward," said Haus. "It is here. It must be here. The sensors said it would be here."

Fahf ah ot nagl'fhtagn lw'nafh. Fahf ah ag lot n'gha.

"The god Beast shall not escape. Not today. Today is the day for revenge."

Pink. Blue. Pink.

Madness! Nothing but utter madness as the brownstone crashed through the nebula's swirling maelstrom.

28

SUDDEN SILENCE FELL OVER everything, like a blanket. A deadening of the chaotic madness which had overtaken everything. The lightning continued to flash electric blue amid the pink, but with the shaking halted, it didn't seem quite so nauseating.

The buzzing stopped in my head too, and the relief washed over me.

I looked up at the window-screen to peer into the eye of the maelstrom. It seemed that the storm formed a thin layer, protecting a quiet, calm sanctuary within.

"We are here, EnterUserName. This must be the Beast's lair."

There was a bright centre to the place, a shining whiteness that hurt to look at. Weren't nebula where stars were born?

"Is that a baby star?" I asked rhetorically.

"Yes," said Haus, who couldn't recognise rhetorical questions. "This nebula is very close to collapse. A new protostar is about to be born."

Orbiting the protostar were several clumps of rocks and dust. They sparkled emerald and gold, jade and silver in the bright light, making a rainbow ring around the newly forming sun.

"And are those planets?" I asked.

"Not yet," said Haus. "They are accretion material. They will be blown apart and scattered when the star is born, but they will likely reform making planets in time."

The place where stars and planets were formed? It was beautiful, breathtakingly magnificent. The outer shell of pink gas crackled again, and blue lightning forked across it. So beautiful. It was full of force and serenity all at once.

"We must prepare, EnterUserName. My scans indicate that the god Beast is here."

The window-screen flashed and showed an image of the harpoon in the attic.

"Hurry, EnterUserName. Put your helmet on and go and get bloody vengeance!"

"Haus, I told you, I don't want to. You manipulated me. You took away my friend, and you lied, and you then made me think I'd caused a suicide. So, why the fuck should I do what you want?"

"You must. For your planet, for yourself, for Rachel, for everyone who died, you must!"

It was useless to argue with Haus. The computer was mad, it had already shown that, and it had killed. So, what else could I do?

Cajoled, I grabbed my space helmet and put it on. The air hissed as it pressurised around me, making my ears pop. Man, I hate it when it does that.

This felt all wrong, but perhaps there was a way out of this madness.

"Hurry, EnterUserName, the Beast is here."

29

THE BEAST APPEARED ON the screen, coming around from the other side of the newly forming sun.

On monstrous, bat-like wings, it circled the star, skirting the proto-corona. Its bulbous, rubbery body bathing in the hot plasma of the birthing sun. From what I could see on the screen, its head was a mass of writhing tentacles, a blubbering insane mess of suckers and hooked claws. It was gargantuan in size, perhaps as big as a moon or small planet; it was challenging to gauge against the protostar.

I very nearly shit myself, and that was from only seeing it on the window-screen at a great distance.

"There it is, EnterUserName, that Beast that killed our world! Man the harpoon."

I scrambled out of the room and stumbled up the stairs, anything to get away from that nightmarish image. On the landing, I grabbed at the cord for the attic hatch, which swung down with a yawning creak. I pulled the ladder down and climbed up into the dusty room.

The attic was lit by only a naked lightbulb swinging from a power cord tacked to a rafter. It cast a dull light, almost nicotine yellow, over the massive harpoon, which took up nearly all available space.

I got into the jockey seat and cranked the big handle, raising the entire harpoon rig.

"Open the attic doors, Haus."

"I can do that, EnterUserName."

The attic roof split down the centre, and the roof opened like a mouth with a tremendous creak and squealing of metal. I cranked the handle more, and the harpoon raised up and out and into the pink and blue space beyond.

I checked down the sights and spied the Beast flying across our bow towards one of the groups of rocks and dust. I drew a bead on it, rotating the harpoon and sighting it as it approached one of the rocks. Its taloned hands outstretched, it grabbed the protoplanet and pressed it against its blubbery abdomen.

"What's it doing?" I asked.

"Scanners show that it is laying an egg in the planetoid," replied Haus.

Everything snapped into place, finally making sense. This wasn't only a stellar nursery; this was the god Beast's nursery too. Some 5 billion years ago, another Beast had laid an egg inside a rock, and that rock had gone on to form Earth. That's some real screwed-up circle of life bullshit.

"We must kill it now," said Haus, "before it spreads more god Beasts."

I took aim down the sights, looking directly at its massive belly. I took a deep breath in, held it. My finger hovered over the trigger...

"Come on, Haus," I said, breathing out. "Let's leave this. It's just an animal."

"It is not," was Haus' reply. "It is a killer. It destroyed our world. It killed Rachel. We must have our vengeance!"

Could you have vengeance against a dumb animal? Was it a dumb animal? There had been words in that weird language in my head. Would an animal have done that? But, even if it wasn't an animal as such, did it even know what it had done? Could it even comprehend? Can an ant get vengeance on a human if the human steps on its brethren?

I sat, frozen in the moment, with the god Beast in my sights and my finger coiled around the trigger.

3Ø

CTHULHU FISHING OFF THE RAO NEBULA

"No," I SAID, FINALLY. And I meant it. "I'm not going to kill it, Haus. I don't think I even could kill it. Look at it, and look at the size of this harpoon. It's not even gonna touch it."

The harpoon was giant, twenty feet long, with a cruel barbed head. The god Beast was the size of a moon. There was just no comparison.

"Then we'll ram that bastard!" said Haus. "Smite it and skewer its black heart, or dash ourselves against it!"

Shit. That did not sound like a good, long-term survival plan.

"Fire, EnterUserName! I will have my revenge!"

I aimed, locked onto the target, and squeezed the trigger.

31

"Goodbye, Haus," I said, getting up from the jockey seat.

The rockets, attached to the harpoon's sides, commenced their firing sequence. I scrambled around, looking for some rope.

My plan was not perfect, not perfect in any sense of the word. But it was 'a' plan, and 'a' plan was better than no plan. Maybe. Ish. Sort of.

I found a decent coil of rope and, hating myself for not having a better plan, did the only thing I could think of to escape.

I lashed myself to the harpoon as best I could.

Yes, it was a dumb plan, a stupid plan, a brain-dead plan. But I was seriously limited on options and time.

The rockets fired, and the harpoon, with me attached, shot out into the pink horizon.

The thunderous sound consumed me, smashing my bones and making me grind my teeth as the G-forces pressed around me. Everything was noise and vibration and just pure weight. And then we were through the artificial force bubble that Haus had made, and we were just flying along in the nebula.

The rockets finished their firing; they were only needed to get the harpoon going. Once in space, there was no resistance, so the bolt would not decelerate.

Slowly, we started to corkscrew as we arrowed our way towards the god Beast, spinning lazily in the pink void. I tilted my head back and looked up at the bolt towards the barbed end. We were flying just as I had aimed.

"Yes! Yes!" came Haus's voice over his commlink to me. "Revenge is mine!"

We shot on. My gasping breaths sounded so loud in my helmet. Was that gunpowder I could smell? No! Don't be fucking stupid! My heart thumped in my ears, a pounding pulse that tried to burst the arteries in my throat.

"I do not know why you have strapped yourself to the harpoon EnterUserName, but I thank you for your sacrifice. Your added weight shall surely pierce the Beast's hide!"

This was a really bad idea, a terrible idea, a catastrophic idea.

I could see the god Beast growing larger and larger as we came closer. It's impossible to say how big it was. Its glowing red eyes were the size of islands; its tentacled mouth was the size of seas. Its bulbous, rubbery belly extended away to continent size, and its wings were as great and vast as the sky.

And onwards towards it, the bolt and I shot.

32

"WAIT," SAID HAUS. "THIS is not right. The trajectory is off. You are missing?"

I had aimed just away from the Beast before firing, targeting the rock it held instead. I had no idea how fast the bolt was travelling, but we were rapidly closing on the creature. It now dominated my horizon.

My breathing was loud in my ears, and I was painfully aware that there was only a thin layer of plastic keeping the atmosphere around my head. That could crack very quickly, and my face would then explode all over space.

I felt pressure on my chest, a vast weight, as I approached the Beast, which got heavier and heavier as I got closer and closer. Was this some kind of gravitational force because of its size, or some other eldritch power? I didn't know, and honestly, it really didn't fucking matter. All that did matter was the agonising crushing on my chest and the fact that it was getting really hard to breathe! I gritted my teeth against the pressure, but it kept increasing. My pulse thu-thumped in my ears. I bit down harder and felt a trickle of blood ooze from my gums and between my lips.

Nightmares reared up in my mind. I was back on Earth in the final moments, but it was always the versions where I died, crushed or burned, or just fell into oblivion. That weight built into a psychic pressure that seemed to emanate from the Beast because it worsened as I got closer and closer.

And the Beast's head roared up before me, a vast continent of rubbery skin, with tentacles as great as rivers. At its centre was a vast, black mouth, filled with rugged teeth as tall as skyscrapers. As the bolt and I shot past the head, the Beast's maelstrom eye turned down to watch.

"No! No! No! Nooooooooooooooooooooooooo!" I could still hear Haus over the commlink.

There were new elements to the nightmares which shot into my brain like trailers for a horror movie. The Beast reached out to grab at me with its hands, its nails slicing through my body, leaving my head just spinning in the pinkish nebula's light. A tentacle encircled me, and an all-consuming pressure squeezed the air from my lungs. I heard my ribs crack and break before seeing nothing but my own exploding blood.

"This cannot be! I will not let it happen!" snarled Haus.

I could feel my depression and terror bubbling inside me in equal measure. What was the point? This thing was just so big. And I was just so small and useless. There was just no way Haus would have been able to get anything like revenge. The bolt that I was tied to would have been only a splinter to something this massive.

I was just a pathetic little ant in comparison to this behemoth. Nothing I could possibly have ever done in my entire life would make the slightest difference to it. Nothing my whole species could have achieved would have even been noticed by it.

"Very well," said Haus. "I shall just have to do this myself."

33

THE BROWNSTONE STARTED FORWARD, edging towards the Beast, but gathering speed.

I could feel the black hole in the basement sucking at me, feeding off my emotions and using that power to drive the house forward. When I had been inside the brownstone, the sensation had just always been there, a constant draining, so small I had never even noticed it. Now, at a distance, although the draining was less, I felt it more. As an insect bite becomes noticeable once scratched, the draining, now lessened by distance, became an irritant as it increased.

The Beast's eye flicked up, away from me, and towards the approaching building. Mountains thrust up as it narrowed its eyes in a determined look. The god Beast recognised a charging opponent when it saw one, even if the foe was minute in comparison. Its tentacles spread wide, and its mouth opened, showing rows upon rows of serrated teeth. It bellowed, but a nebula is not dense enough for the acoustic sound to travel. Where the sound should have been was just vibration rumbling around me, buzzing in my helmet.

The bolt and I shot onward, down the Beast's body. Its massive rubbery stomach was directly above me, juddering and rumbling with its bellowed cry. Its wings outstretched; great bat-like leather things covered my horizon, turning it seaweed green.

Then the bolt hit its mark, striking into the small planetoid clutched in the Beast's hind claws. The barbed head buried itself deep into the rock, causing spiderweb cracks to zig-zag across the surface. I felt the impact judder up my body, making my bones rattle and ache.

Finally, I freed myself from my rope attachments and slowly dropped to the surface. This planetoid appeared to have some minor gravity, even though it wasn't much larger than the brownstone. Whilst overhead, the abdomen and tail of the great god Beast flashed across the sky as it charged at the flying house.

"Come at me." I heard Haus say on the intercom. "Come on, I'm right here. Come on!"

The black hole increased its pull on me as Haus used the energy to accelerate. My knees went weak, and I slumped awkwardly to the planetoid's surface, panting and coughing.

"More power!" cried Haus. "Faster! I will have my revenge on the Beast!"

The ground beneath me cracked and broke further. The latticework of fissures from the bolt's head radiated out, crisscrossing the planetoid's surface. Glowing pink goo seeped up from the cracks, spilling out like erupting lava. It flowed over my hands, and I felt the warmth of it – it felt alive.

What had Haus said? This wasn't just a stellar nursery, but the Beast's nursery too. So, that would make this an...

The ground split under me, and a tentacle slithered its way out, grasping, twisting and spooling at nothing. Another tentacle burst out, and another and another. Tentacles as thick as me, but twice my height, writhed and groped around me. The planetoid's crust shifted like the eggshell it was, and I stood splayed across a drop. I saw, within the fissure, a gigantic golden eye staring back at me. It blinked lazily, then shifted beneath the crust, showing me only rubbery phlegm-coloured skin.

"Onward! Onward! I will smash you to pieces, you bastard!" cried Haus over the intercom.

I staggered again as more emotional energy drained from me. I was running out of time.

34

THE NEW PLAN WAS almost as stupid as the last one. In fact, I'd go so far as to say it was probably stupider, but I really was out of options.

"Here, Haus," I shouted. "Have it all! Have all my pain, my fear, my depression. Have the whole goddamn pointless, lonely universe!"

And, I let it all go – all of my negativity flowed from me, like a river, and went straight into the black hole.

My loneliness, the pointless days spent drinking, accomplishing nothing and falling further and further into a spinning routine of emptiness. My cowardice, running away in the face of the monster that destroyed my planet. My excuses: it was too big, it was too much, why me? My self-pity.

"Ah yes! Thank you, EnterUserName! More power!" said Haus.

And the black hole sucked it up as an infant feeding off its mother, it drank and drank and drank, but it could never be sated.

It took my hatred of myself, my feelings of not being good enough. It slurped up my niggling doubts and the voices in my head.

"Wait, too much power! I can't control the flow of the energy. It's increasing at an exponential rate!"

As the last blackness left my body, I felt that link, the tether, between myself and the brownstone snap. And it was all gone, every last bit of it, and I was free to make my way in the universe.

I jumped down the fissure onto the back of the embryonic Beast. Its hide squished beneath my boots in a soft, gelatinous way. As I clung to its back, I could see that the planetoid was a hollow egg.

The little god Beast was balled up inside, rolling over itself in an endless loop. Its arms and legs were stunted and still had webbing between the digits. It had a long tadpole tail which swished and shucked as it tumbled about in its eggy domain. Its eyes were enormous compared to the rest of it; they bulged out from its head as if they were stuck onto its skull rather than being an internal part. Slung underneath its flabby belly was a gigantic egg sack, with a deep orange yolk still inside.

There was a probing in my mind, a feeling of someone rummaging around in my most inner thoughts. It was an inexperienced fumbling, I felt, as if whoever was attempting it didn't really know what they were doing.

The feeling of words came, as they had before from the god Beast. Only this time, they were cruder, making even less sense, as if a toddler was communicating.

Tiny, insignificant plaything should get off. Not allowed. Too early. Not ready to play.

"Come on, you stupid baby," I hissed. "I have to leave, and you're the only way out."

Breakable toy, make laugh. Go away. Too early.

The thing was too young to be reasoned with. I clambered over its belly, swinging down to the egg yoke slung beneath it. I grabbed the umbilical connecting it, feeling an unpleasant, warm, mushy sensation as I held it. I scrambled back up its rubbery flanks and onto its thick neck, which was the width of a car. I'd pulled the umbilical along with me, and I looped it under the Beast's throat.

I pulled on this new choke chain, and the embryonic god reared beneath me.

"Stop! Stop, EnterUserName; what have you done? We're redlining!" said Haus over the intercom, still trying to wrestle with the insane amount of power I'd pumped into the black hole.

I geed my new mount, and the little god Beast smashed its way out of the planetoid it had been using as an egg, leaving shards of broken rock in its wake.

35

LOOKING BACK OVER MY shoulder, I could see the great god Beast charging at the brownstone. Its vast, green bat-like wings were outstretched, and its hands reached forward to grab and smash the tiny house as they jousted towards each other.

"All systems are at critical. I am unable to redirect all this power. It's gonna blow!" said Haus.

Shafts of painfully bright light shot out of the windows as the energy spiked.

"Fuck you, EnterUserName! Fuck you and that dragon! I'll save you both a seat in hell!"

The brownstone detonated in a blinding flash and concussive wave. Fire and debris exploded out in a thin ring, setting anything it touched alight.

The god Beast's hand hesitated as it reached out. Its wings flapped in what looked like panic as it tried to halt its charge. But it was already too late.

At the centre of the exploding ring, which had until a few seconds before been the only home I had known for years, was a small, black spot. It was blacker than black, not just an absence of light but a blackness that drank light. And, slowly, but steadily, I watched it expand, sucking in the matter around it.

I recognised it, almost instantly, the rapidly expanding black hole of my depression.

"Oh shit!" I said and spurred my little steed away, out towards the edge of the nebula.

The great god Beast seemed frozen, staring at the enlarging black hole, its hand still outstretched.

Even a god Beast has to obey the laws of creation.

Its hand started to stretch, pulled inexorably towards the event horizon. That seemed to break the Beast out of its stupor, and it drew back its hand. It turned, powerful muscles in its shoulders working, flapping its great green wings, trying to get away.

Get away was what the embryo Beast and I had to do. So I pulled at the umbilical choke chain, and my steed sped up, away from the black hole. I could feel fingers of gravity pulling at us, trying to entrap us and drag us back down into the vortex.

The black hole grew, gorging itself on the gas and rocky debris contained within the nebula. Each atom it ate increased its mass, increasing its gravitational pull, which sucked in more and more and more. Its event horizon, the black ring around which even light could not escape, crackled and sparked as gases combined and ignited, looking like the firey entrance to hell.

The inescapable gravity well already had the Beast in its mouth. The great god's foot started to stretch, its long, cruelly sharp toenails elongated, distending out towards the black hole's heart. Its mighty wings flapped, and its arms outstretched, but it was trapped, falling into the void.

Its foot disappeared as it crossed the event horizon. Then its shins, its knees, its thighs, its rubbery belly, its wings, and head. Finally, its outstretched arms were all that was left beyond the yawning chasm. Then, it was gone.

36

MY EMBRYONIC STEED AND I rode on out into space. The outer layer of cosmic storm, which had previously surrounded the nebula's heart, appeared to have been blown away by the detonating brownstone. The Iraq Nebula was no more.

Behind us, the black hole continued to grow, feasting on the nebula's gas and rocks, but we were now at such a distance that I could only feel a slight tug from it. Finally, we were out and away from immediate danger.

The feeling of words came again into my mind as the little god Beast communicated.

Tiny thing, am tired. Too early. Out not good. Light not good. Very tired.

My Beast steed slowed down in the starry void. His immature wings flapped heavily, and his chest was rising and falling in great heaves.

Too tired. Too early.

His big bulging eyes rolled at me in what looked like pleading, but there was nothing I could do.

"I'm sorry," I said. "It is my fault. I birthed you too soon, and you weren't ready. I did it because I wanted to live, and I didn't care what happened to you. I will have to live with that."

Unhelpful, tiny thing. Tired now. Scared. Fear.

"You shouldn't be afraid of death," I said, as I caught the scent of gunpowder once again. "It is not the monster some imagine it to be. It's just a door to what is beyond."

I don't understand, I heard in my brain. And then the little god closed its eyes and never opened them again.

And I was left alone amongst the stars and dust and the smell of gunpowder; the last orphan, the lone survivor, in a now godless universe.

For the first time, in what seemed like forever, I laughed and laughed. And I just kept on laughing.

About the Author

Chris Meekings is a writer from Gloucester.

Several of his works have appeared on Bizarro Central's *Flash Fiction Friday*.

His bizarro novellas, *Elephant Vice* (released in 2015 via Eraserhead Press), and *Moon Mayor* (released 2022 by Hybrid Sequence Media) are unquestionably things that he wrote .

His novel, *Ravens and Writing Desks,* (released in 2016 by Omnium Gatherum) is also a thing that he wrote.

He is a founding member of the British Bizarro Community who recently released the anthology *The Bumper Book of British Bizarro,* all profits of which go towards the Mermaids Trust.

None of his works have appeared on toilet walls.

He is currently 58 weasels in a trench coat, just looking for love.

Other Titles from Planet Bizarro

Peculiar Monstrosities – A Bizarre Horror Anthology
A stripper's boyfriend bites off more than he can chew during a hiking trip. A man looking for love marries a jukebox. A popular children's character is brought to life, but something isn't quite right. A shady exchange on a Kaiju cruise leads to catastrophic complications. Peculiar Monstrosities is packed with fourteen exquisitely crafted stories from new and established authors of Bizarro fiction. Featuring tales by: Kevin J. Kennedy, Zoltan Komor, Shelly Lyons, Tim Anderson, Tim O'Neal, Gregory L. Norris, Joshua Chaplinsky, Stanley B. Webb, Jackk N. Killington, Kristen Callender, Michael Pollentine, Tony Rauch, Mark Cowling, and Alistair Rey.

Extremely Bizarre – A Bizarro/Extreme Horror Anthology

A lonely man gets more than he bargained for after ordering a hand-in-a-can from an old magazine. Enter a world where face pareidolia is deadly and one mistake can lead to a horrifying death. Join a traumatized woman as she returns to the place of her son's death, looking for something to fill the hole in her life. Extremely Bizarre is an exquisite collection of ten tales accompanied by detailed illustrations. Expect extreme horror. Expect bizarro. Expect therapy. Featuring tales by: Robert Guffey, Shaun Avery, Sergi G. Oset, Kevin J. Kennedy, T.M. Morgan, Irene Ferraro-Sives, Cliff McNish, B. Patrick Lonberg, Todd Love, Melanie Atkinson, and Gerard Houarner.

Sons of Sorrow
by Matthew A. Clarke

SOME THINGS ARE BETTER LEFT ALONE Henk has been living a relatively carefree life in the city since fleeing the horrors of the town of Sorrow with his brother, Dave. Never would he have dreamt of returning. Not even for her.

But time and banality have a funny way of eroding the memory of even the worst experiences, bringing only the better times to the forefront of recall, so when he receives a wedding invitation from the third part of their old monster-fighting trio, he finds himself unable to turn it down.

Sorrow has changed drastically from the place it once was, with the murders and suicides that once plagued the town being used as a selling point by wealthy investors to turn it into a morbid attraction for dark tourists.

Beneath the costumed mascots and smiling families, is all really as it seems? Or by returning, have Henk and Dave inadvertently awoken an ancient evil far deadlier than anything they've faced before?

Sons of Sorrow is the latest bizarre horror from the mind of
Matthew A. Clarke.

Porn Land
by Kevin Shamel
OH, NO, PORN IS ILLEGAL!

That's right. Porn stars are criminals, pornographic websites are
being systematically destroyed, and not even softcore or selfies
are okay. And that's just in our world. It's literally destroying
the magick city of sexual expression—PORN LAND!

Phil and Zed, arriving through magickal means and ill-equipped
for adventure, must travel through the erotic metropolis and
gather pieces of THE PORNOMICRON—a sexual spell-book
that bridges our worlds. And it won't be easy. They'll have to get
past a giant geisha and her samurai army, a determined detective
who's after their asses, a badass dominatrix and her gang, a
bunch more sexy people, a bunch of unsexy people... And even
more things that will freak you out and make you horny—like
a sperm monster and ambulance sex. Will Phil and Zed put the
book together, save Porn Land and their new friends, *and* make
pornography legal in our world again? (Yes. It'd be a stupid story
if they didn't. But it's *how* they do it that you'll want to read
about.)

It's a story about sucking, *and* not sucking. It's got hardcore sex
and a hardcore message. It's ridiculous *and* you'll wanna rub
one out to it. It's freakin' PORN LAND, BABY!

Weird Fauna of the Multiverse
A trio of novellas by Leo X. Robertson

— A gimp becomes mesmerized by the koala at a zoo on Venus.
She draws him into the battle between the purebred animal

supremacy of the park's hippo owner and the anti-establish-mentarian koala uprising. — In a godless future, a rich Martian traveler hunts the former Vatican—now a hotspot for sex tourism—for his deceased wife. When he discovers a dead priest in the streets, he begins to investigate the weird plot of the city's head cyberpope. — Supercats spend their days responding to rescue calls across their city. Since there aren't enough rescues to go around, one supercat decides to do something drastic and devious to resolve this crisis, changing the industry forever. The stories of *Weird Fauna of the Multiverse* explore what happens to love and work when pushed beyond the boundaries of human decency.

A Quaint New England Town
by Gregory L. Norris

When Ezra Wilson took the job as a census worker, he never imagined it would lead to a place like his latest assignment. From the moment he turns off the interstate and travels past the village limits, it becomes clear that Heritage isn't just some quaint New England town. A sinister encounter at an automobile graveyard is only the start. In Heritage Proper, a town divided down the middle both politically and literally, Ezra is met with hostility on both sides of an imposing brick wall that separates warring factions that have maintained a fragile peace. After scaling the wall into Heritage North, Ezra discovers a beautiful young woman held prisoner in a fortified basement room and promises to help her. To do so will expose the last of the small town's dark secrets and lay bare big planetary dangers if Ezra survives his visit to a destination where even the white picket fences are not at all what they appear to be.

CTHULHU FISHING OFF THE IRAQ NEBULA

Russells in Time
by Kevin Shamel

Because you can never have enough Shamel! In this novella, a trio of recognizable characters find themselves travelling back in time and in the middle of a heated battle between the dinosaurs and a race of giant land-squid. Who will they side with? And will we get to see Russell Brand kicking ass in an Iron Man-esque suit? (Spoiler — yes. We totally will.)

Selleck's 'Stache is Missing!
by Charles Chadwick

Celebrated Hollywood star Tom Selleck has it all: talent, good looks, a winning personality, and a track record of television and movie hits, enjoyed by millions around the world. Until one day, while filming his latest project, an old rival attacks him and steals his mustache. Now, lost and adrift, Tom struggles with his new life. Along with a group of dedicated crew members, celebrity friends, government agents, and the robot voice of an old co-star, he has to find the strength to take on his greatest role ever: tracking down his old rival, retrieving his legacy, and saving the world.

Songs About My Father's Crotch
by Dustin Reade

My father's crotch sang many songs, and the first of them all, was me.
Now it is my turn to sing, and I will sing to you of many things. Here are my stories. Here are my songs.
I will sing of a man who wrestles furniture, and of a sister who disappears.

I will sing of modern day cannibalism, and Dwayne Johnson's elbow.

I will sing of foul-mouthed butterflies and plastic sharks, and I will hum a few bars about cartoon trains.

I will warble on about beards, sentient houses, monsters and Roald Dahl.

But mostly, with this collection of short stories, I will sing songs about my father's crotch.

Bizarro outsider, Dustin Reade, presents eleven stories of weirdo lit, culled from the deepest recesses of the human imagination, and sprinkled with thoughts and flakes from other parts of the body as well.

Don't miss it. Or do. Whatever.

The Secret Sex Lives of Ghosts
by Dustin Reade

Thomas Johansson can see ghosts after a near death experience, and has made a living killing them for a second time. After discovering that being possessed by a ghost causes an intense hallucinogenic effect, he goes into business with a perverted dead man named Jerry, selling possession as a street drug (street name: Ghost). But is the farmhouse he sees while possessed really a hallucination? Or is it something else?

Dad Jokes
by Justin Hunter

A deviant kid tires of his absent father's antics and summons a curse that will kill him the moment he tells one of his tired zingers. Little does he know that this time, his dad has left for good.

The curse spreads. Dads are dying all over town and nobody knows how to stop it. Meanwhile, the wayward father kills time at a strip club and meets a dancer whose body hungers for wayward men. Literally.

The town falls into chaos while their lone police officer's sentient shotgun begins to question his owner's monogamy.

Fiona, the kid's sister, tires of her mother's inattentiveness, and decides she must take her freedom, and the town's future, into her own hands.

DAD JOKES by Justin Hunter is a comedic action-packed adventure about a small town horror and a deadly curse that could spell the end of humanity.

The Falling Crystal Palace
by Carl Fuerst

The residents of Sterling, Indiana don't know who they are. Sixty-one year old Tory Stebbins runs an Identity Verification agency that can help. But, as her town implodes, so does her business. She has fewer clients, stiffer competition, and her methods have become mysteriously ineffective. Most alarmingly, she's now suffering from the same problems she's helped her clients with over the length of her career.

Just when her situation seems beyond hope, Tory receives a cryptic message from Hoppy Bashford, her best friend who, forty years earlier, disappeared. "I don't want to say it's a life or death situation," writes Hoppy, "but I want to say it's a life or death situation."

Tory's quest to find Hoppy leads her through the strange, shifting landscapes of Sterling, and the enigmatic quarry around which it is built, and ultimately to the Crystal Palace Resort, a hotel and waterpark with an infinite maze of hallways, rooms, and bizarrely themed attractions whose size and scope defy physics and reason. To locate her lost friend, escape from the resort, and find a cure for the identity-scrambling, reality-bending condition from which everyone in her world suffers, Tory must come to terms with who she is; she must determine her place in, relationship to, and path through the universe.

Dead Monkey Rum
by Robert Guffey

A mixture of urban fantasy and Los Angeles noir, *Dead Monkey Rum* revolves around a stolen Tiki idol that contains the ashes of visionary artist Stanislaw Szukalski. Our heroes, an alcoholic monkey named Robert McLintock and a beautiful bartender named Stephanie Waterfall, must locate the missing statue in the wilds of Los Angeles before a tribe of pissed-off Yetis can get their massive, dirty paws on it. Because the obsidian idol possesses magical properties, the Yetis want to use it to kickstart the destruction of the human race, thus paving the way for the cryptozoological beasts to take humanity's place as the rulers of Earth.

Ebola Saves the Planet! and Other Wholesome Tales
by Matthew A. Clarke

A man gets a ticket to a popular gameshow and is willing to risk life and limb to go home with the prize. A family tries to survive in a world where gravity is reversed and explosive balloon animals rule the streets. A new epidemic hits the world. People are spontaneously erupting into mounds of steel coils, but after years, the kids are growing restless. Will they be able to survive a secret outing outside of their safehouse? A young girl born to super villains feels out of place among her family and peers. Upon discovering a dastardly plot to cause widespread catastrophe, will she defy her family and save the planet? Ebola Saves the Planet! and Other Wholesome Tales is a collection of eleven wild tales (and illustrations) from the mind of Matthew A. Clarke.

Troll
by Matthew A. Clarke

"A horror filled look at the reality of the damage internet trolls can cause, with a touch of bizarro." Kevin J. Kennedy, author of *Halloween Land.*

Scotty is no stranger to being bullied, but after a chance encounter on an online chatroom, finds hope in Rebecca.
Scotty is about to find out that people on the internet can be worse than people in real life.

Facebook. Twitter. These are the places the modern troll thrives. How far would you be willing to go to bring a troll to justice?

Ingram Content Group UK Ltd.
Milton Keynes UK
UKHW042048190323
418673UK00004B/123